Pirates!

adapted by Jane E. Gerver • based on the story by Magnús Scheving
written by Noah Zachary, Cole Louie, Ken Pontiac, and Magnús Scheving
illustrated by Howard Simpson

Ready-to-Read

SIMON SPOTLIGHT/NICK JR.
New York London Toronto Sydney

Based on the TV series *LazyTown*™ as seen on Nick Jr.®

SIMON SPOTLIGHT
An imprint of Simon & Schuster Children's Publishing Division
1230 Avenue of the Americas, New York, New York 10020

Manufactured in the United States of America
First Edition
2 4 6 8 10 9 7 5 3 1
Library of Congress Cataloging-in-Publication Data
Gerver, Jane E.
Pirates!/adapted by Jane Gerver; illustrated by Howard Simpson.
—1st ed.
p. cm.—(Ready-to-read)
"Based on the story by Magnús Scheving written by Noah Zachary, Cole Louie, Ken Pontiac, and Magnús Scheving."
"Based on the TV series LazyTown as seen on Nick Jr."—T.p. verso.
ISBN-13: 978-1-4169-4064-7
ISBN-10: 1-4169-4064-2
I. Scheving, Magnus. II. Simpson, Howard. III. LazyTown (Television program) IV. Title.
PZ7.G3264Pi 2007
2006032334

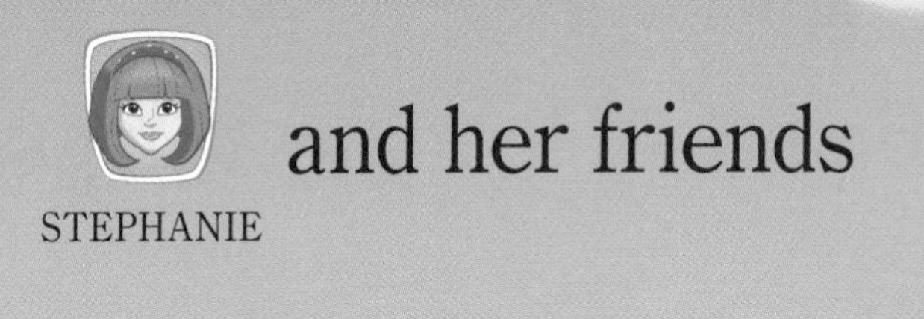

STEPHANIE and her friends

were playing pirates.

"There once was a real PIRATE

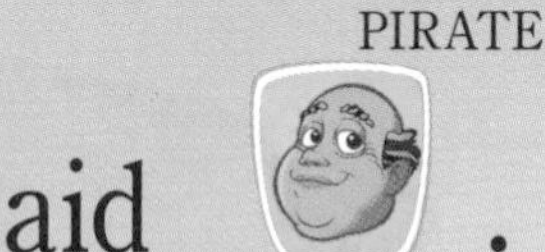

in LazyTown!" said THE MAYOR.

"His name was Rotten Beard."

"Rotten Beard stole many things,"
said THE MAYOR.
"And he broke the LazyTown STONE!"

THE MAYOR

showed the STONE

to the kids.

On the STONE were the words:

The rest was missing!

"The missing part is in

a  ,"  said.

TREASURE CHEST THE MAYOR

"One day someone will find it,

and we must do what it says."

"Aha!" said ROBBIE ROTTEN.

"I will make a fake STONE.

Then everyone will have to

do what I say!"

ROBBIE ROTTEN made a fake STONE

and put it into a TREASURE CHEST.

"Now I just have to find

my  BEARD and  EYE PATCH."

The kids wanted to find

the old .
TREASURE CHEST

Instead they found a !
PIRATE

“I am Rotten Beard,”

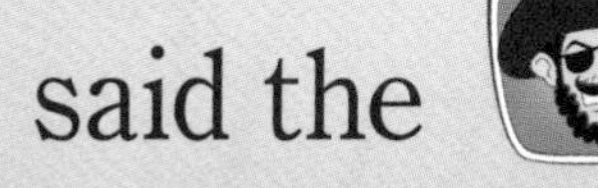
said the .
PIRATE

"I have a MAP and a SHOVEL, but I need you to help me find the TREASURE!" the PIRATE said.

He gave STEPHANIE a MAP.

The kids followed the MAP

to the town square.

STEPHANIE dug up a TREASURE CHEST!

There was a STONE inside.

“It is the missing piece!”

said STEPHANIE.

THE MAYOR

joined the two pieces.

Now the said:
STONE

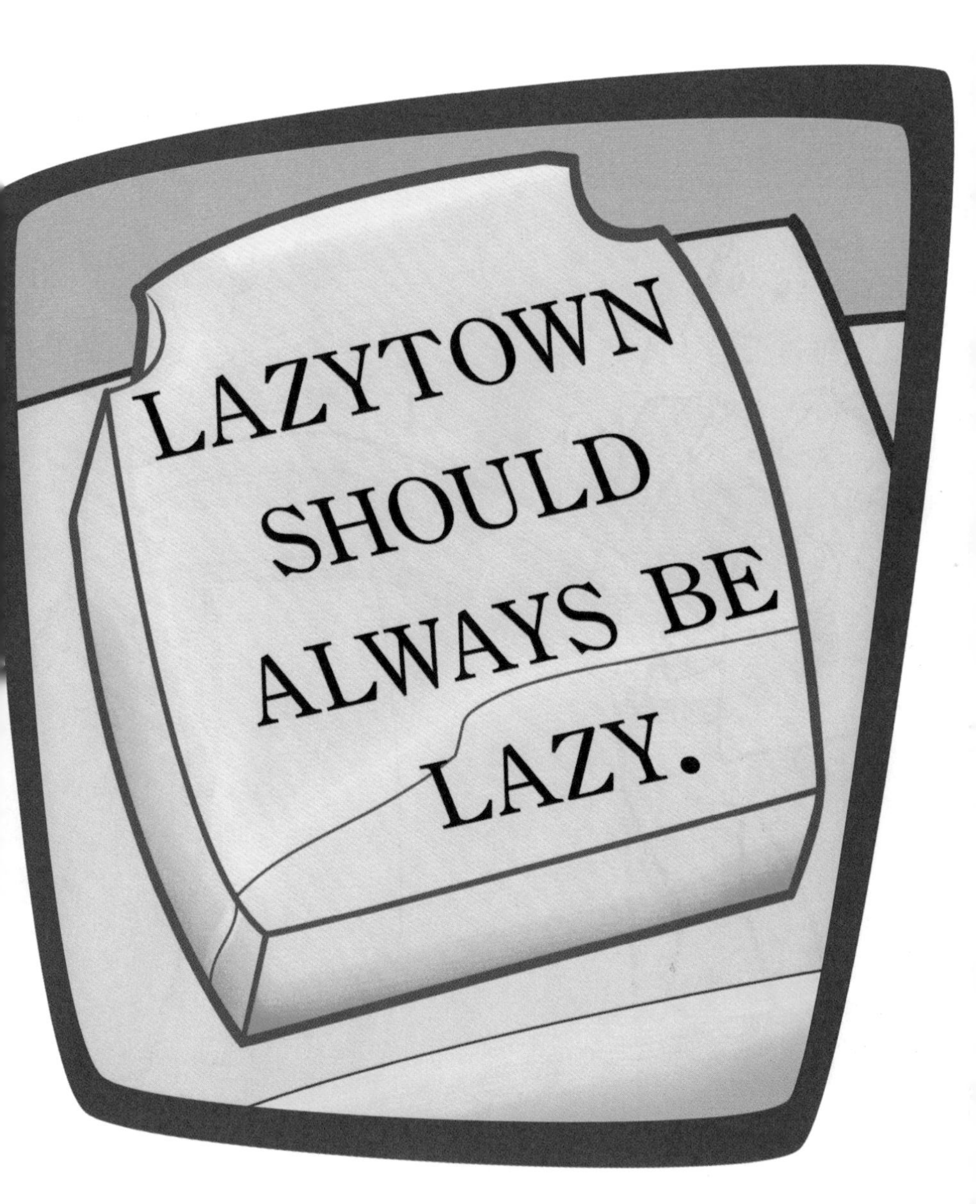

"We have to do what
the STONE says," THE MAYOR said.

"Then I can't dance anymore!"

STEPHANIE

said.

Everyone was sad.

STEPHANIE leaned on the STONE.

Creak! The STONE opened.

There was a MAP inside!

The kids followed

the new MAP.

They found another TREASURE CHEST!

ROBBIE ROTTEN

heard the kids.

"Those kids are not lazy!

I must stop them!" he said.

The PIRATE tied the kids

to a TREE.

"Help!" they cried.

SPORTACUS

came to save them.

He threw the 
TREASURE CHEST

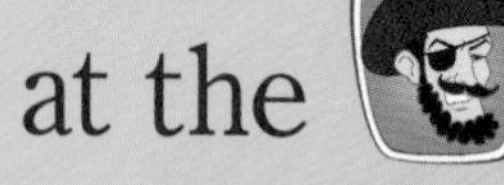
at the .
PIRATE

The PIRATE fell into a hole!

His BEARD and EYE PATCH came off.

"It is ROBBIE ROTTEN!" the kids said.

opened the 

.

There was a STONE inside.

joined the two pieces of 

.

Now the  said:

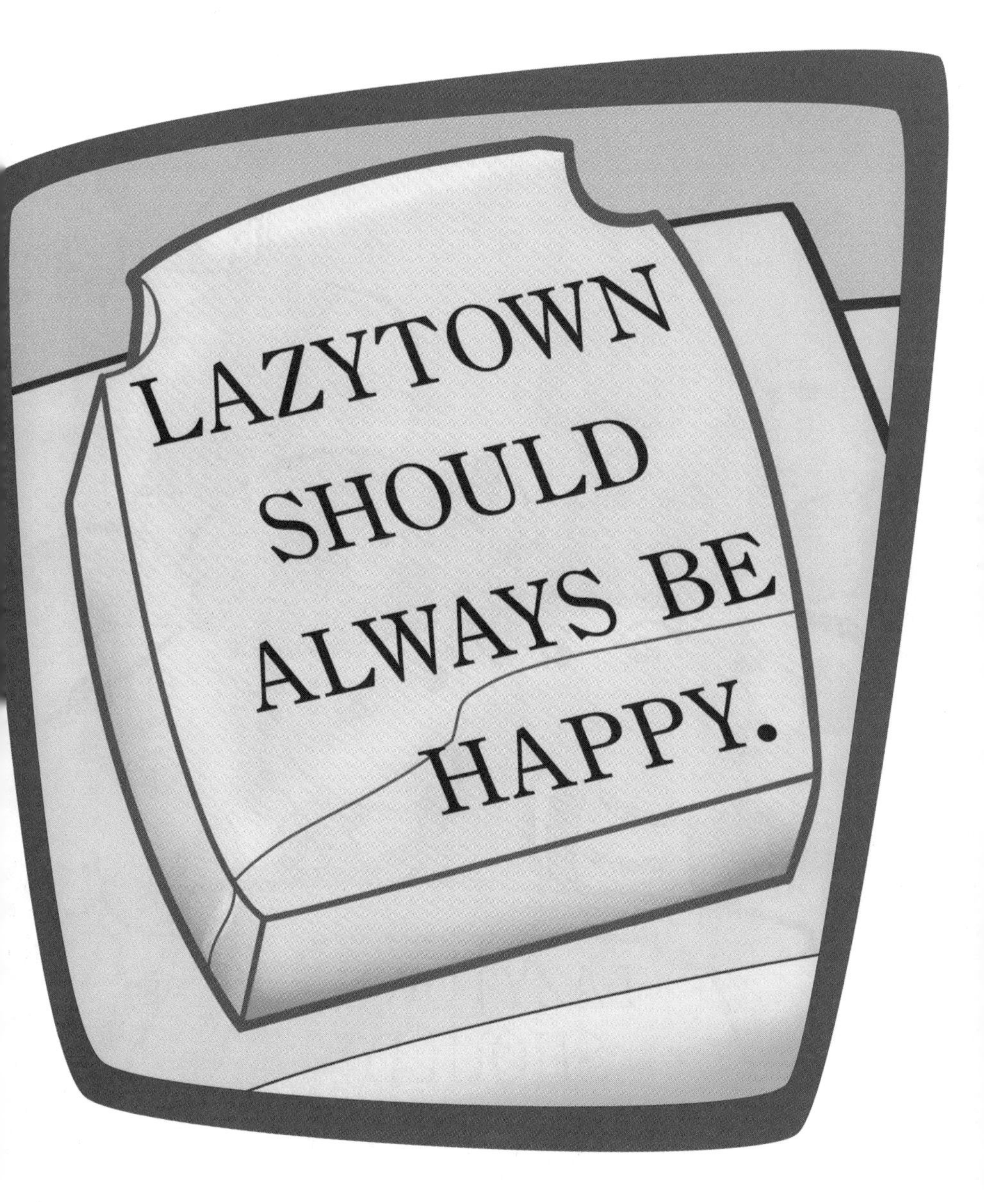

"That is easy to do,"
said THE MAYOR. "Just smile!"
And they all did—
except for ROBBIE ROTTEN!
LAZYTOWN
SHOULD
ALWAYS BE
HAPPY.